I Can Be Anything

Dona Herweck Rice

I can be a pilot and fly a jumbo jet.

I can be a farmer with a chicken for a pet.

I can be a writer who writes the books you read.

I can be a grocer who sells the food you need.

Apples
Tomatoes

I can be a doctor and fix your broken bones.

I can be a banker and give out building loans.

I can be an actor with a hit show on TV.

I will do a good job,
whatever I choose to be.